Shadows on the Wall

written by Pam Holden
illustrated by Jane MacDonald

Can you make shadow
pictures on the wall?
Put your hands like this.

What does this shadow picture look like?
What could it be?

It's a bird with big wings.
Look! It's flying away!

4

Put your hands like this.
What does this one look like?
What else could it be?

It could be a dog or a wolf.
Look! It's barking at you.

Make your hands do this.
What could this shadow
picture be?

It's an elephant with tusks.
Look at its trunk swinging.

Put your hands like this.
What does this one look like?
What else could it be?

That's a tortoise or a turtle.
It's walking slowly away.

Make your hands do this.
What could this picture be?

It's a rabbit with long ears.
It can wiggle its ears.

Put your hands like this.
What does this shadow
picture look like?

That's a deer with big horns.
What else has horns?

Put your hands like this.
You could make a goat.
It has horns and a beard.

Can you make a duck like this?
What else can you make
with a shadow?